A Peace of Edith

Toy Taylor

By Toy Taylor
Printed in the U.S.A
Printed ISBN: 978-1-7335685-6-2
EBOOK ISBN: 978-1-7335685-7-9
Published by: Toy Taylor
Publication: February 2019

Anariah Kaye, I love you baby.
Your brother loves you baby.
The world is yours; stay focused.

Prologue

Edith is a typical teenager in New York. She is in the middle of her junior year of high school. Like most she has friends, does extracurricular activities, and is active in other areas. Life is good for her.

As we transition from teenagers to adults, life starts to take on a more realistic form. Life seems like a playground before those years of transition take shape. Some playgrounds may be richer than others. Some playgrounds may be tougher than others. Regardless, we all experience the freedom of childhood.

Edith's parents had afforded her a great life. She wanted for nothing. She was top in her class. She purposely did things and completed academics with her own future in mind. Her parents set a great example for her.

Like most young adults, she begins to experience life turbulence as she grows into an adult. We meet Edith as life turns contentious for her. She goes from a life of having it all in the city, to having little in the country with her grandparents.

Instead of things getting better with time, they get worse as she worries about the previous problem. She steps into self-realization as each problem unfolds. Before, her parents took care of her problems. They were her heroes.

Their mortality is revealed to her the older she gets. They become less dependable. She learns they do not live by the standards they hold her to. She has to cope with their past decisions, as well as, her own.

Her friends and family are a strong support system for her. Support is no permanent shield from life. Some truths will get through. Some hard lesson have to be learned no matter how much support a person has.

Edith will reveal her resilience as the story unfolds. She will have to be honest with herself when no one else around her will. She will have to accept things she does not like.

What she will not do is remain stagnant while everyone around her is paralyzed by problems.

Chapter 1: The Overdose

I was 17 when I realized my mom already knew my dad had a drug problem. I explained what I had witnessed in grave detail and shock. I was shook. There was whole school lesson on not "doing drugs" thanks to sober minds. Lessons that that resonate with generations.

She stood still as a statue, and warm tears rolled down my face in the December storm outside. I explained to her that he was rocked back in his recliner, breathing, but unresponsive. As I called 911, I noticed a needle on the side table with a small glob of black goo. All I could think as the first responder was asking me questions was, "I wasn't supposed to be home".

I told my mom that the first responders rushed into our brownstone without regard. That was why the door frame was tethered. Her face never changed. Her stare never left me. She only blinked when I said the word "I".

I told her my relief when the paramedics were able to revive him. They possessed some potion, they shot it in him, he woke up. I apologized to her they would not let me in the ambulance because I was a minor. We were taught family first, I thought I had left him hanging. As I grew older, I realized he left us hanging.

When I finished my monologue, so full of zeal, concern, defeat, she simply said,

"I am sorry baby."

She turned and walked away. I realized she knew. She knew because she did not react. My mom was a reactor. She was the ultimate reactor. Yet there was little response to what would be the most powerful shift in my life.

"Mom"

My mom did not break her glance from the front window, "Yes babe?"

"Are you going to see dad?" I hesitated because I was unsure of her emotions. I had never seen her like this.

She paused for what seemed like an eternity and said slowly, "No".

My mom was always up for questions, but as I said, she is a reactor. I chose my words carefully when I asked my next question. I considered her hurt after I realized she knew. I did not want to further a painful cause.

"Mom, I will only ask one more question."

"Go ahead my love."

"What was type of Dr-."

"It was heroin."

I could see a tear roll down her face through the window's reflection. I left her there to bear the weight of whatever emotion she was bearing. I did not want to. I wanted to hug her. I wanted her to hug me. I wanted to understand it all.

I retreated to my bedroom and shut the door. I collapsed into my bed and cried for a while. I cried for me. I cried for my mom. I cried for my little sister who would eventually come home to the somberness.

She was trapped at my aunt's house thanks to the storm. We were trapped at home. I cried a little harder. I walked through my front door celebrating I was able to make it home before the storm hit. I walked into my living room and discovered my unconscious father. My mom had told me to stay in safe at my best friend's house until it passed.

I cried a bit more. My mom always said I needed to listen more. She says sometimes there is good reason to heed good instruction. Today her words were as clear as the truth I witnessed. My father was a drug addict. I cried until sleep took it's turn in my life for the day.

Everything about the next morning said my life had changed. We were a pretty rambunctious family. I was used to waking up to someone's music, be it classical, gospel, or jazz. On weekdays, the aroma of an imported coffee bean brewing would tickle my nose as I woke.

If my mom woke me up, it was stern and militant. "Edith, Edith." Is all I would hear and I had about 5 seconds before the covers were ripped from my bed with a "Good Morning." Mom was the house timekeeper.

She did not allow the morning pleasure of asking for more time in bed. When mom says something, it is almost always an imperative. Even "Good Morning."

When I was younger, I saw my mom drag an older cousin from the bed by an ankle. This happened after my mom said "Good Morning" twice. I thought it wise to always get up on the first one after that. That cousin still spent many nights in my home after that incident to my surprise.

If my dad woke me up things were different. He'd kiss you a few times. He would wiggle your nose or ear. You could smell his aftershave and toothpaste above the imported coffee beans. He was a lover. He would check on me and see what I needed.

After our talk, he would leave me to get dressed. He then would wake my sister. Her morning almost never went well. She was daddy's baby girl. She almost never took well to being woken up.

My mom and dad had a pact. He was responsible for waking her up and getting her ready every morning. This pact happened after my mom left her at home multiple times with my dad for "wasting her time". In plain English, my sister either pitched a royal fit or ran around the house until my mom was late. I think my mom would leave the Pope before being late.

This morning was cold. Cold because my dad had not switched the heater on after we slept. We slept with the house cool in the winters. My dad would wake up before everyone, warm the brownstone, and start his routine.

My body was weak, but I crept to the thermostat. The heater began to roar almost immediately. I walked towards my parent's room to check on my mom. The king size bed was empty when I arrived. So was the bedroom.

I began searching the house. I immediately became so anxious with negative thoughts I did not think to just call her name. I found her in the kitchen with her back to the opening. This was unusual. My mom always sat at the island facing the opening of the kitchen. It was her spot. She was sitting in my dad's chair.

Relieved to see her, I hugged her. She hugged me back, but her hug was different. My mom even hugged with authority. This morning, her hug seemed to need me more than I needed it. I hugged her tighter. She let her body go limp in my arms.

My mom looked horrible. I mean that in the most loving way. She was a judge. I almost never saw a hair out if place on this women before 9 pm. I admired everything about my mom. She was who I wanted to be. This morning my hero was in need of saving.

There was no book, phone, or document in front her. There was no imported coffee brewing. This was different. We were not allowed to sit with much ideal time. My mom had a "either you are researching or creating" rule. She said, "the ideal mind was the devil's workshop". She modeled that very rule herself. My mom was always up to something. Today she was a cold statue in my father's chair.

My muscles were relaxing due to the brownstone warming up. I don't remember meeting my mom without caffeine. There was a strange woman in my kitchen wearing my mom's skin. She was creepy. I started brewing coffee in hopes of getting my mom back.

I grabbed her a blanket. She was shivering. I thought my mom may have snapped. Before I could consider not having to healthy parents anymore, the coffee machine's beeping broke my train of thought. I added her French Vanilla creamer and a drop of hazelnut extract to her cup of coffee.

It was my first time making her coffee. I had watched her do it a million times. My mom was not one to need much assistance. She was like the house warden. We were not concerned with her needs, we were busy meeting her expectations. But a warm and loving warden, if we were not being loud or arriving late somewhere.

She watched the mug for a strange time. She picked it up slowly, blew it to cool it, and took a sip.

"Thank you, baby girl," she managed to get out after her first sip.

"You are welcome mom." I said back with a warm smile.

She drank her coffee some more. She still had not relaxed. But she seemed a wee bit more alive. That helped ease my anxiety.

"Mom."

"Yes."

"What or where, maybe I should ask how, can I contact dad."

"You can't access him right now," she would not make eye contact.

"Why", I asked confused.

She put her coffee back on the island. She kept her stare on her mug for another strange minute. I have never seen this woman lost for words. This has to be bad.

She looked at me. For the first time, in the eye. The strange lady in front of me had no eye lashes or eye brows. A sure sign she had lost it. Her eyes were more swollen and red than mine from crying over night I presumed. Yet she was still beautiful.

"Edith."

She paused for a very long time.

"Edith, your dad has been checked into a rehab facility." Her voice cracked while her lips formed the word rehab. "He will be in a state of detoxing, for a while. I will let you know when it is ok to speak with him." Her blood shot eyes went back to her mug.

My mom's heart was broken. More broken than mine. I had more questions, as always, but I did not want to drag her through the hurt of yesterday. Or the days to come as so she had put it.

The storm was still whistling outside. Not as loud as last night. It seemed to be subsiding. New York winters could be rough, but the view after it blankets our world with snow is beautiful. We were not going anywhere anytime soon.

I cut on my mom's favorite jazz record and played it on the brownstone speaker system. If we had to be here, we could at least relax. I started my day as if yesterday did not happen. A snow storm may have closed school, but it did not excuse us from the assignments.

I grabbed my backpack from my room and returned to the island. My mom was in the same spot. With the same cup. With the same stare. I hugged her again, sat down with her, and began my studies.

My mom took a deep sigh. "Edith."

"Yes ma?"

"Do you remember the business trip your dad took about two years ago? He was "out of the country"," she said slowly.

"Yeah, Milan, right? He brought us back some nice key chains and souvenir hats. A marketing conference." I responded.

"Your dad was never in Milan. He was in a Florida rehabilitation center."

Someone's cell phone began to buzz in the background almost instantaneously with the ending of her sentence. She asked me to retrieve her phone, in case it concerned my baby sister. As I walked to get the phone I thought about the lie my parents had told. I was recoiled at the length they went to cover it up. I wondered what else they had lied about.

It was indeed her phone. The call was from my aunt, my aunt that was housing my sister. My mom retreated to her office to speak with my aunt. It was located at the back of the house. It was understood if she went there, she needed privacy or quietness. It was her cave.

I tried to resume my studies, but her sentence had me distracted. I retrieved my own cell phone from my room. I had not checked it since I had found my dad. There were tons of messages and social media notifications. Most of them from my boyfriend.

Drew was my first boyfriend and my current boyfriend. We started dating when we were 13. We broke up often and made up always. I'm sure he was worried I had not responded. Were hardly went a few hours without contacting each other.

His messages signaled his worry. I wanted to rush and call him back, but I had no words to say. My dad was a top marketing executive at a well-known firm in the city. I was forbade from telling my family's closest secrets to an unforgiving world. My mom explained "it takes a million things to build a good reputation, and one thing to tear it down." So, we kept our toughest times in house as a practice.

I sent him a text hoping he would not call, but he did. I ignored the call and told him we had a family emergency. I did not want to go through his series of questioning. I had enough on my mind. He could be quite a butt hole sometimes.

He replied with a few unhappy face emojis and told me to call him soon. I assured him I would, then went straight to social media. I needed a distraction. I was careful not to like or comment on any social post. Drew would perceive it as time I could have used to talk to him.

As I scrolled, I still thought about my parents. Most of my timeline was littered with cliché snow day post. My friends were sledding and enjoying the day off. I was wondering how many more times my dad was on some camouflage business trip.

Chapter 2:
The Start of
Recovery

It had been 3 days since I found my dad when I was woken by a thunderous noise. That noise was my baby sister. My aunt was dropping her off and they were making all types of commotion in the family room. I could hear my sister was happy to see my mom.

That made me happy for my mom. She needed my sister's spark. She was so much like my dad with her little self. I decided to brush my teeth and welcome her home. I needed a little bit of her spark too.

I tried to sneak up behind her while she was distracted by my mom. However, when my aunt Julia saw me, she instantly grabbed me and hugged me tight. She whispered she was "sorry I was going through this". She hugged me a little tighter before letting me go.

When I tried to whisper "thank you", my baby sister heard me and turned around. Juju had thick curly hair like my mom. She had a perfect nose and almond eyes like my dad. She favored him a lot. I was the spitting image of my mom.

Juju jumped from my mom's arms into mine. I missed that little nugget those three days. She brought a new light, we desperately needed, into the house. She squirmed and moved the way a 5-year-old does when they are excited.

She missed me and asked, "What was I doing without her?"

I kissed her back and told her how much I missed her. I stole a glance at my mom who was occupied with my aunt. She looked back to her usual self. I could not tell if it was a show for my aunt or not. At least she looked like she was normal again.

The last few days had been hard. I knew they were about to get tougher. I tried to imagine going back to my normal life, my day dreaming came to an abrupt stop. My sister said what we all feared,

"Where is daddy?"

My mom covered her mouth and began to sob. Without words, my aunt lulled my mom to her office. I took the baby to my room.

I was doing my best to distract my sister. Sadly, I was distracted myself. Distracted by the weight of what my dad had done. I was distracted by the way my mom responded. I was distracted wondering what we would tell my sister. I knew it was a matter of time before she asked again. My goal was to just occupy her as much as I could.

"Will you give me red?" Juju said breaking my concentration.

"What?" I asked once I realized she was trying to get my attention.

"Red paint please!" She said with a smile.

She was so untainted by the current calamity that has fallen upon my family, I kept having to remind myself "she does not know" before I responded sullenly. I struggled between being the protective big sister and the emotionally distraught daughter most of the time we painted. Part of me wanted to keep my sister occupied to give my mom time. Part of me wanted to break down in the arms of anyone at this point. I turned on some saxophone infused jazz on my room speakers to even the temperament in the room and in my head.

The music helped me keep my mind on painting with Juju until a particular song came on. There was a saxophone solo that reminded me of my dad. He introduced me to most of the jazz pieces I knew. He made a point to drag our family to countless concerts in efforts to "culture" us. He mandated that we participated in the arts on a regular basis as to not "lose our poise of exposure".

He said you could "always tell how narrow a person was by where they have not been" While I day dreamed about my dad, my phone vibrated loudly on my desk and interrupted my thoughts.

When I picked up the phone and realized it was my boyfriend I put it back down. I did not have the capacity for his usual prying. I understand that I was leaving him in the dark about our current family emergency. When I thought about our last conversation, it became apparent to me why he had such a sense of urgency. I had put him off the last three days to tend to my mom. I needed the next few days for my baby sister and myself.

For what seemed like the next 10 minutes my phone vibrated excessively.

"Well aren't you going to answer it?" Juju said disturbed from her precious paintings.

"No."

"Why not?"

"Because."

"Because what? You do not want to talk to whoever it is?"

"Right."

"Why?"

"Because I already know what he wants."

"So, it is a *he*?"

"Juju, don't be a nosy bug."

"Ugh, ok sissy." Juju conceded.

I began to worry about Drew though. This was the longest we had gone without talking. Besides the break ups. I thought he would probably break up with me for sure since I won't have real reason for my absence. I must admit, he was being quite pleasant. Probably since our last conversation.

We painted, danced, watched TV, did anything we could on a cold December afternoon. While I kept my sister occupied, I could hear my mom moving around in the kitchen. I heard pots rattling and cabinets closing. I was hoping she was preparing food for us, I had lived on sandwiches and cereal waiting for her to return to life. I was grateful to eat, but craving a real meal.

My mom was an amazing cook among all the other things she was extraordinary at. It was like she had the Midas Touch. Outside of my personal opinion, we hosted lavish dinners and gatherings for family and friends. My mom would not allow a chef in her kitchen. She prepared grand meals she did not have the luxury of enjoying. I think she became full from the compliments of her dishes she prepared that night.

"Sissy I am hungry." Juju broke my roving thoughts again.

"Me too. You want to go see what mom is doing in the kitchen?" I said with a smile.

"Sure!"

"Let's clean up first. That will be the first question mom asks before she has us wash up to eat."

We cleaned up our activities and put away our supplies. The aroma of my mom's choosen dish made my heart warm in a way it had not for a few days. I washed our hands and got us table ready before we entered the kitchen. As we headed towards the kitchen, I heard my mom speaking with someone. My guess was she was on the phone, I was sure my aunt had left.

"-yes I. I really do not have an answer right now, it is too complicated." I heard her say as we headed toward the kitchen. Her tone was soft, like she cared for the person. I decided it had to be my dad and sped up our pace toward the kitchen.

"I do love you, I just-" she said before I interrupted.

"Mom is that dad?" I asked in haste. It had been a few days since I heard his voice live. I was excited. My mom was clearly startled. She dropped her cooking utensil and quickly hung up the phone. My heart dropped as I watched her scramble to press end.

"Daddy, Daddy, Daddy!" Juju chimed in to bring us back to focus.

"That... that was not your father girls. Set the table please," she said in a low tone. She would not make eye contact with me. She recovered her cooking routine and resumed dinner. I chose my next words carefully because my mom was a wordsmith. I wanted to know who she was talking to. I also knew she was not one for prying.

I moved to the cabinets to retrieve plates. I sent Juju to grab our eating utensils. I drummed up the courage to ask my mom what was on my mind. I decided to wait until we sat at the table.

"Mom."

"Yes love?"

"You were talking to someone the way you talk to dad. Who was that?" I said incredulously.

She paused. Then she said, "I am not married to you dear. Those are questions I simply can refuse to answer when you ask." She then turned her attention to my little sister and inquired about her stay at my aunt's.

There she was. There was Judge Geaux. She was moving around and witty again. I was glad she appeared to be better. I just wanted to know who was on the other end of the phone. I conceded that I would not find out tonight.

I could hear my cell phone vibrating on my desk in my room. I knew it was Drew. The storm had subsided. The snow was melting. I would see him soon. I decided to wait and face him at school.

Chapter 3:
The Package

My first day back to school after my dad's overdose was a welcomed distraction. I was ready to catch up with my friends. I did not speak with them much over the impromptu break. I was so focused on my family that my friends were not a priority in my life for a change.

I know that Drew would be looking for me too. The last time I heard his voice we had agreed to become more serious. The next thing I remember is finding my dad. I am sure he thinks I got cold feet. I still didn't know what to tell him for going missing. He would just have to settle for it being a private family matter I thought.

I maneuvered through friends and listened to stories of how everyone spent their time during the storm. I wanted desperately for class to start because I had no exciting news to share. When I was asked what I did, I just mentioned spending time with my sister to pass the time. Which I did if one thought about it.

When the bell finally rang for instruction to begin, I felt relieved. As I scurried to class, I did think it was odd that Drew had not shown up at my morning "spot". My friends and I had a morning ritual in the same spot unless a school function forbade us. Whenever he was looking for me, he usually would come there.

As I walked towards Pre-calculus, I saw him and a girl, I knew wanted to date him, tucked in a corridor. They were standing close enough that you could tell the conversation was private. She handed him a small brown package. Right after, she leaned in towards him, and my heart sank.

I thought she was going to kiss him, but she whispered in his ear. He smiled and pushed her back by her arms. Then he paused. I stood there long enough for him to feel my eyes pierce him. He instantly pursued me once he met my gaze. Thankfully, my class was a few doors from the corridor.

My Pre-calculus instructor was not a very nice lady either. I knew he would end his chase at the threshold of her door. And he did. I do not know if he stood there or not. I would not look at the door area until I heard it close.

My phone began to vibrate excessively as class commenced. I thought it was best to power it off. Mrs. Mach would have taken pride in confiscating it. Our school had a "no cell phone" during class policy. We were only allowed to use them in common areas.

If it was confiscated, the only way to get it back was to do extra duty for the teacher or pay $40. Most of our parents gave us that amount as a daily lunch allowance. So, paying mostly took precedence over manual labor. The school used this to their advantage.

Each cell phone collected by a teacher rewarded them a third of the proceeds to class supplies. She was paid to take our cell phones in the name of education. That was not enough. She also promptly told our parent if we breathed too loud.

My mom showed up to school enough after a call that I would rather her not. Plus, Drew had evidently moved on. It hurt to think about it. However, I had bigger problems than him. I had not seen or heard from my dad in almost two weeks. It was easy to forget about Drew when I thought about my dad.

I spent most of Pre-calculus staring out of the window. Being a statue was about the only way to be unengaged and not break a rule. I was wondering if my mom had lied. Maybe it was my dad on the phone that evening before dinner.

Mrs. Mach called my name to end my endless thoughts. I jumped and asked her to repeat her question. She paused to signal her annoyance with me. Then she repeated the part of the problem she wanted me to solve. We both know she called on me because I was not paying attention.

After I finished with my answer and explanation, I looked at the clock. We had 5 more minutes before class ended. I was hoping Drew had another obligation besides waiting at my classroom door. I was in no mood to talk to him. I kind of welcomed the idea he had someone else to talk to with all the calamity in my family's life.

The bell rang and we waited to be dismissed. Normally I was like a pressed springboard waiting to hit the hallway. I hoped she took her time letting us go this time. She let the class go, but she asked a few of us to stay back.

She explained she was not pleased with the quality of work we had submitted during the storm. I would normally explain myself and make claims of doing better. Instead, she reminded me of seeing my dad once the storm started. Once we were dismissed my stomach dropped. I just knew Drew would be waiting. It made him upset when I ignored him.

My arm was grabbed at my elbow as soon as I walked away from my classroom door. I did resist, but he tightened his grip. I knew if we made a scene it would be investigated regardless. Instead of attracting the attention, I decided to give him the four minutes we had in between classes.

"Can I explain?" He said still holding my elbow.

"I don't care." I said nonchalantly.

"It is not what it looked like." He pleaded.

"I am pretty sure of what I saw. I am also very aware of who I saw you with. You enjoyed it." I smirked. "May I go to class?"

"I was getting something for you. I was just sloppy with it I guess." I could tell he was remorseful.

He then went into his backpack and pulled out the brown package I saw the girl hand him. I looked at it for an awkward second and then he handed it to me. I was hesitant to take it. He held it out to me until I did. As I reached for it the tardy bell rang.

"Please cut your phone back on." He whispered in my ear before he dashed off to class.

I stood there looking at the package. I didn't know what to think. I considered opening it, but it was best to avoid the tardy sweepers. I took a back way I knew to Art. Mr. Carpenter was cool, I knew he would let me in.

Once I settled into class, I decided against turning my phone on. It would make a thousand vibrations that I would have to scurry to cut off. I thought it was rude. I was already late to the man's class. I asked to be excused to the restroom once the pace of class slowed down.

"Mr. Carpenter."

"Yes mam? What may I do for you?" He was always so pleasant.

"May I use the restroom?"

He frowned slightly, "No time during the extra time you spent in the hallway mam?"

Now we had the class's attention. Most of them saw me with Drew. Most of them knew I saw Drew with another girl. I was only going to the restroom to turn on my phone. I suddenly felt awkward.

"Never mind sir." I said to end the show.

He softened, "You may go. Next time I suggest you have your priorities in the right order." He motioned his hand toward the door.

I was careful in the hallway because I did not want to run into Drew. I also had to be fast. Someone could "mention" Drew's girl was in the hallway. He would bee line to figure out why and where. I took my cell phone out once I reached the restroom door.

My head was down as I entered, I was powering up my phone. My next task was to turn the vibration off and head back to class. I had no real interest in the bathroom. Not until my ears heard a certain voice before I looked up to see a certain face.

Rocki. Rocki. Rocki. The heifer I witnessed whisper in my boyfriend's ear earlier. I kept my concentration on my phone even after I heard her voice. I just could not believe the universe was after me at school too. I planned to completely ignore her and walk out of the restroom.

I had a reputation for being stuck up at school. I was not. My mom simply taught me to exert energy where there was profit. This profit could be spiritual, mental, or physical. Conversation with Rocki appealed to possess none of the aforementioned. But then she said something that caught my attention.

"Did you like it?"

I paused and gave her the respect of eye contact. "Like what?"

She was smiling now. This is someone I rarely gave the opportunity of existing in my life. She showed her teeth like it was an audition. "Oh, maybe he has not given it to you." She said and continued to apply mascara.

"Give me what?" Now I was inquisitive. She knew something I did not. About my boyfriend. Or at least I assumed. She never identified "he".

"Nothing. Forget I said anything. You have a good dude though. Shout out." She closed her mascara as she said this. By this time my phone was shaking like crazy. I was receiving all of the notifications I neglected when I turned my phone off.

I simply said, "Thank you."

Then I turn to walk out of the restroom. I returned my silenced phone to my backpack as I crossed over into the hallway. I was now interested in want Drew had to say. I was also interested in what was in the brown package he handed me.

When I returned to class, my peers were making their things tidy for dismissal. I joined in and followed suite. It was time for lunch next. I knew Drew would be there and would want to talk. I still had neglected to read all the messages he sent because of class and Rocki.

The bell rang and I headed toward the cafeteria. This time my elbow was grabbed, but with a little force. It was Drew again. Annoyed that I had not responded via phone.

"Man did you see my messages?" He said in a hushed, but aggressive tone.

"No. I did not. I was only in class." I retorted.

He did a small circle where he stood. Signaling he was choosing his words. "Man did you open my gift?" I could tell he was trying to control himself. Drew kept a perfect facade at school like he was a political figure. Then again, he was the son of a political figure.

His dad was the deputy mayor. This made him my mom's boss and a client at my dad's dentistry. Drew and I had a long history. Our parents were old college buddies.

"No. Did you think I was rushing to open something I watched your girlfriend give you?" Boom. He was mad. He walked away and went to eat with his friends. Once he gave me some space, I was able to open my phone and ready my neglected notifications.

His last message read, "I can't wait until we feel each other on the next level. I hope it is soon." I all of a sudden felt bad. He had been pouring his heart out to a phone that had no receiver for hours this morning. Rocki confirming I had a "Good dude", made me think I did see something wrong.

I was now curious about the brown package. I took it from my backpack and opened it carefully. I looked around to make sure Drew was not watching me. As I finally tore the last piece to expose what it was, Jana pushed me from behind and said "what's up stranger?"

I had not told her about the big decision that Drew and I made to take things to the next level. Even though she was my best friend, I was cautious of what information I allowed people to carry about me. I put the package away and ate lunch as the rest of my friends arrived to "our table". I thought about Drew and the package during our lunch rant. However, I thought it was best to open the package in private.

Chapter 4: The Move

When my aunt Melissa dropped me off at home, I rushed to my room. I thought it was strange that my aunt Melissa, my mom's youngest sister, had picked me up without notice. The anticipation of what was in the package blurred my immediate vantage point. As I brushed past the family room, I was halted from my scurry.

I reversed my steps without turning around. All of my aunts, with the exception of my mom's oldest sister Gina were at my house. The only time they were all together was for a holiday or a family tragedy. I spent the day at school, so it definitely was not a holiday.

Their presence trumped my thoughts of the package. Their visitation had the vibes of a tragedy call. My aunt Julia was consoling my mom. My aunt Tangie noticed me come back. She rushed to obviously keep me going towards another part of the house.

"Hey love how was school?" She was attempting to distract me. It might have worked on Juju.

"What's wrong with my mom?"

"Umm. I think it is best if she talks to you about it." My aunt hesitated.

My mom heard us talking. We were in a hallway connected to the family room. Before the space could become awkward between my aunt and I, my mom managed to yell, "Just tell her Tang, I have been trying to for a few days." I then heard her resume her sobbing.

My aunt and I both watched the wall on the other side while she was talking. Once she finished I turned my attention back to my aunt. I felt she was going to confirm my worst fear. My dad was dead.

"Tell me what auntie?" My eyelids refused to blink until she said something.

"Edi."

My name was not enough. My eyelids stood their ground.

"Edi, we have to pack the house up?" She said quietly.

"What?" Now I was completely confused. The last time I came from school I found my drug comatose father. Then, my first day back, I was being told I had to "pack up my house". I was for sure these broads were pulling a prank on me. They had to be. This was the only house I had ever lived in.

"Your da-... Your mom needs us to pack the house up. That is why we are here." Tears began to fill her eyes.

"Pack up the house? Where will we live? Where will we take our belongings that we pack?" I began to ask specific questions.

Instead of answering, my aunt let her tears fall and walked away. I followed her into the family room. I found a place to sit and mourned with them. I had no clue what was going on. It evidently was not good.

My aunt Julia finally let go of my mom and said, "Well Cheri, we have to do a what we have to do. I have already told you we have homes here. You have made your decision." Everyone began moving about the house. Cleaning, packing, and singing in harmony. I did not move.

I could not decide if I was sad or upset no one was being honest with me. I was super thrown off by my aunt's comment, "we have homes here". I went on a hunt for my mom to ask questions. There was no point in piecing a story together and the leading role player was in the house.

I found my mom in her study. She was slowly packing. She was the only sister not singing. When she felt my presence, she stopped to acknowledge me. We hugged for a while and then she started talking without cue.

"Edith, we are moving to Texas. Your dad's rehabilitation expenses are too much of a burden when only I am bringing in income". Her heart was heavy.

"Income! We are moving to Texas!" Where will you work there!" I had lost it. This is the reason that my aunt would not break the news to me. I do not blame her. I felt my parents should explain.

"Edith," She motioned her hand for me to calm down, "Baby girl, I have a job in Texas. Your grandfather was owed a favor, an old frat brother of his moved me in as a candidate on short notice." Slow tears were falling from her eyes.

I did not want to hammer my mom for what my dad did. I just asked, "When are we leaving?"

"We fly out Sunday night".

"THIS IS MY JUNIOR YEAR OF HIGH SCHOOL!" I flipped again. I ran through the house calling for my aunt Julia. Surely, I could stay with her. My mom and dad did this not me. They did not consult me as if I was a little kid.

"Aunt Ju! Can I stay here in New York with you?" She was a middle aged real estate broker with no children. She had plenty of room. Before she could muster up an answer, my mom entered the kitchen where we were. My aunt was packing dishes.

"Edith." My mom called.

I kept my gaze on my aunt. This was not right. Surely, she knew it. She even exposed there were other options.

My mom walked over and positioned herself between my aunt and I. She looked me in my eyes and said, "Whatever you do not pack will be sold with the house. Your fit will not be tolerated. You can go to your room voluntarily or I can drag you there. You are being disrespectful. Things happen. You adapt."

I knew she would indeed drag me, so I went on my own. I officially hated my mom, my dad, and my aunts. They just stood there and watched without trying to help me. I also wanted to know where my sister was. Now, I had no one in the house to ask. I hated them all.

I thought about Drew as I marched unhappily to my room. I instantly wanted to talk to him having no allies in my house. When I made it to my room I plopped on my bed and cried. I could not believe my dad. I could not believe my mom. All I wanted was Drew.

Thinking of him directed my thoughts back to the package. My backpack was still somewhere in the front parts of the house. I had to decide if that package was worth facing the people who just saw me be embarrassed by my mom. I considered that Rocki had a hand in it, and my suspicion outweighed the ridicule of my loved ones. It was not funny now, but it would be at family functions to come.

Luckily the part of the house I needed to access was empty. I found my bag in the hallway my aunt Tangie told me I was going to move. I retrieved it and returned to my room. There it was. Where I had left it. The brown package my boyfriend had shared with another heifer.

When I opened it, I cried again. This time tears of joy. It was the Hermes wallet I mentioned I liked while we were out shopping. He remembered.

It also had my name bedazzled on the back. Rocki. She was nortorious for customizing personal items on campus. Now their little sneak meeting in a corridor made sense. I instantly felt bad and called Drew.

"Hello." he sounded annoyed.

"Thank you for my gift." I said still feeling bad for giving him a hard time.

"Glad you finally found the time to notice it." He was short.

"Drew I-"

"Hey I have to go I'm doing something with my dad." He said hurriedly.

"Ok." I hung up the phone and admired my gift.

Chapter 5:
The
Announcement

The morning after my mom's big moving announcement, I found it hard to get out of bed. Part of me wanted the move to be a dream. Part of me wanted my dad's overdose to be a dream. I just wanted the life I had had weeks prior.

After accepting my reality, I contemplated playing sick. I rarely missed school. After a few days, it would no longer be my school anyway. I had not spoken to my mom since I was dismissed from the kitchen. I did not want to reopen our communication with a lie. So, I just conceded to getting ready for school.

I also had another motive for going. I needed to tell Drew about our move. I could not bear telling him over the phone. Especially after being such a snob about the Rocki situation. I owed him an explanation face to face for my strange behavior.

I wondered how he would feel about us after I told him. We agreed to take things to the next level together. Now I was faced with telling him I was moving across the country.

Not because of happy family tidings. Because my dad was a selfish heroin addict.

After getting dressed I had to find my mom. Thinking of my dad made me think of her. After sleeping on my emotions, I realized I was not being fair to her. My dad being a heroin addict meant her husband was a heroin addict. I should have had more compassion when I got the news.

When I opened my room door, the aroma of bacon eased my anxiety. I was excited to eat my mom's cooking. I was so upset the night before I failed to eat dinner. The smell of her biscuits was intoxicating.

There was one weird notion. She never made a big breakfast before school. They were always prepared on weekends when she had more time. Regardless, I was grateful as I headed to the kitchen.

The sound of her voice met me before I made it to the kitchen. The tone of her voice stopped me before I entered. It was soft, again, like she was talking to my dad. I stopped to listen instead of interrupting this time.

"-I do not think that is possible. There is enough going on." My mom said and then paused as to listen.

After the long pause she said, "Have some consideration for my wishes, just as I had consideration for yours all those years ago. If I had not, we would not be having this conversation. Now is not the time to tell her. Please respect that."

I considered who she was talking to. Last time she said it was not my dad. I still wondered if it was him this time. I really missed him by now. I wanted to talk to him; addict or not.

My feelings overwhelmed me and I rushed into the kitchen. My mom's back was to me and she was at the stove. I caused her to drop the phone she was holding between her ear and should with my rushed entrance.

"Mom is that dad?!"

"No honey, are you hungry?" She said picking up her phone and returning to food prep.

Now I was undoubtedly confused. If not my dad, then who? Who's is "her"? Now is not the time to tell "her" what. I felt so indifferent. I wondered if there were more surprises besides Texas.

My mom seemed to be in good spirits. I knew prying into her phone call would change that mood. Instead I asked about or move and specifics. Something I should have done the night before.

"Mom, can I ask about our move?" I asked shyly.

"Yes, you sure can darling." She said.

"Like, where are we going? I suspect I will have a new school, but where? Where will we live when we get there? Please do not say Grandma and Grandpas-"

"Edith. We will live with Grandma and Grandpa. You will attend my old high school. I know it seems like this all happened so fast. The truth is, dad and I were having financial issues because of his drug use before he went to rehab. The overdose did not start the moving process. It simply sped it up."

"But mom-"

"It is time for school Edi. You still have a few more days to spend with your friends. I need to get your sister up and off to school." She said halting my questions.

"Ok mom." I decided to finish eating and go instead of pressing for more answers. I needed to talk with Drew anyhow. My stomach became knotted when I thought about telling him I was moving. It was either tell him, or disappear. He meant too much to me to just disappear.

When I got to school I set out to find him before the first bell. When I found him, he was getting tutoring. I knew I would have to wait. I headed to class to talk to Jana about the move. I decided to just tell everyone my dad was sick.

Jana was in the athletic pod where I expected her to be. She was with Beth and Kennedy, two of our other friends. I felt myself get anxious as I approached them. They met me with their usual salutations.

"Waddup Edi! Why so blue doll?" Beth said lovingly.

My anxiety took over. "Hey guys. I just. I mean. Uh nothing." I did not have the courage to tell them.

"Alright. Well we are here if you need to talk." Jana said to save me. They could all sense my weird vibe. They just did not know the cause.

"You guys going to Rebecca's party Saturday?" Kennedy said to change the subject.

"I am," said Beth.

"So am I," Jana chimed in behind her. "It is about to be lit!" She did a little shimmy to show her excitement.

Kennedy then turned to me, "what about you girlie?"

I hesitated. I knew I was flying out Sunday. I was sure I would be helping finalize the move. Still, I had a little hope. Maybe it could be my last night out with Drew.

"Uh I have to check with my mom first," I said unsure.

"Cool. Well if you all want, we can go shopping for outfits after school Friday." Jana added.

The word "shopping" made me nervous. My mom said we were moving because of financial issues. I wondered was the issue too big to get a new outfit. There was just one question to ask first. I had to find out if I was allowed to go the night before we were due in Texas.

As always, saved by the bell. The first class bell rang before I had to commit to a shopping spree. The thought of shopping made me wonder how broke we really were thanks to my dad. I had seen broke people before. I was just not used to being one of them. I decided to talk to my mom before I committed to my friends.

On my way to class, Drew grabbed me just as I was walking inside.

"Hey beautiful, long time no talk." He said sweetly.

"I know and I am sorry. Can I meet up with you at lunch?" I was hoping he would take being pushed off again well one more time.

"Yea, sure. Just wanted to catch up with you. I saw you come by during morning tutoring." He said with a smile.

I gave him a hug and headed into class. It was hard for me to pay attention while there. The move. The party. Drew. It was all too much to digest. I was starting to feel the pressure of telling everyone I was leaving.

Time flies when you dread things. I am sure of it. Lunch crept upon me like a thief. I had spent most of the time before, deciding if I would tell Dre what really happened to my dad.

I wanted to be upfront with him. I did not want to broadcast my family's plight.

Especially since our families were so close. My mom always warned me of mixing personal business with business contacts. Thanks to their positions, our parents were friends, as well as, business contacts.

I could not eat. The thought of talking to Drew stressed me out. I was hoping he would understand. He had been pretty pleasant lately. I was glad about that. He possessed quite the temper.

When I sat down he had not made it to the lunch area. I waited at a small table we sat at when we did not eat with our friends. I figured he was grabbing a bite. I took out a book to bide my idle time.

Just as I got into my chapter, I felt a tap on my left shoulder. When I turned to look no one was there. I knew it had to be Drew standing over the right shoulder. "Hey miss lady is this seat taken?" He said in a thick southern accent.

He sat down with his plate of a cheeseburger and fries. I took a sip of his sweet tea.

"Hey now, that will cost you." He said jokingly.

"What is the price? I got a new Hermes wallet I can trade you. It is customized too!" I replied sarcastically.

"Na, I need more than that." He said as he shook his head.

"Really? What exactly do you have in mind?" I teased.

"Hmmm, maybe that thing we were talking about a while ago." He paused to wait for my response.

I knew exactly where he was going with the conversation. Quite frankly I was just scared to go there with him. I still had not even told him I was leaving. Now was the time.

"Drew I need to tell you something." I said quietly.

He could sense my mood and got serious himself. "What's good baby?"

"You have to keep it between us. I haven't told anyone yet."

"Don't I always?" He questioned.

"My mom just told me we are moving." I waited for his reaction.

"Moving where? Why?" He asked inquisitively.

"Texas, my dad is sick. We are moving with my grandparents."

He did not respond immediately. He stared into the open as if to daydream. He crossed his arms and uncrossed them a couple of times. Then he took his index finger and rubbed it against his head as if he was thinking.

Suddenly he exploded. "So, you are just going to leave me?

There he was. There was my boy brat. He rarely took kindly to news he did not want to hear. There was the reaction I had anticipated.

"I did all this stuff for nothing? When did you find this out?" He was livid.

"Shhhhh you are making a scene," I said looking around at the attention we had drawn.

He got a grip of himself and finished eating in silence. Before lunch was over he said, "What does that mean for us?"

"I don't know," and I really did not.

"When are you leaving?"

"Sunday."

I gave me a piercing glance and said "Stay here. With me."

"I already tried to stay with my aunt. My mom would not allow it, I have to go."

He grabbed his things and stormed away. I let him go. Class would start soon. I did not want to upset him further. I figured he would reach out once he calmed down.

And he did. Later that night after school he sent a message that simply said "Thinking about you." I replied in excitement. We did have a fight, but I wanted to hear from him. I would fly out in days. I did not want to spend that time fighting.

"Hey you," I replied back.

"What are you doing," he asked.

"Waiting on you to call me."

"For what, you are trying to leave me."

"I think you understand it is not my call."

"Can I see you before you go? Like away from school?" He inquired.

"Yea, when?" I asked.

"Tonight. I can come over when your mom goes to sleep." He pressed.

"Not a good idea. Let's hang out after school tomorrow." I was not risking my mom catching us.

"Can we take things to the next level tomorrow if I wait?" He was like a hound.

I had just gotten him to calm down. Instead of sending him in another frenzy, I replied, "Yes."

Chapter 6: The Next Level

Tomorrow came faster than I had anticipated. As school dragged along, I began to wonder if I still wanted to go to the next level with Drew. I felt like I loved him. However, I was super nervous.

When the final bell rang, I considered making a dash home and blaming my mom. There was just one problem. I was not the best liar. My memory was not sufficiently developed to keep up with fabrications. Since my mom was a judge, I was trained to spot them.

I agreed to meet him by the gym so we could catch a train together. He did not live far from me. I did not live far from friends. We agreed to ride the train for discretion.

Taking things to the next level was a hot topic amongst my friends. If they saw us going home together, I knew what they would assume. A part of me did not care. I was leaving for infinity in a few days.

A part of me wanted to keep my secret a secret. I knew it would eventually get out. It was not much of a secret if a second person held the information. I trusted Drew to keep it to himself for a small while.

Realistically, I knew he would eventually tell his friend. Who would then tell their friends. Who would then talk about it with my friends. I was lucky enough to have my mom explain that no secret was really a secret. She said, "After all my years in the justice system I learned one thing. A friend will tell, that never fails."

Despite knowing this truth, I still decided to do it. I cared about Drew a lot. If I was going to do it with anyone, I wanted it to be him. As I stepped on the train I decided to let my anxiety go. I made up my mind to let it happen.

I forced my mind to think about Texas instead of us. I had been to Elgin before, but it was not for me. There were cows and dust everywhere. The air was nice, but the number of weird people saying "y'all" was unbearable.

"You nervous baby?" He asked as we came closer to our stop.

"Yea." Was all I could manage to say. My mind was all over the place from realizing my dad was a heroin addict, to the Texas fruit flies I would be combatting soon. Being with Drew was a welcomed distraction. What we were about to do just added to the calamity already present in my mind.

The train brakes interrupted my thoughts. It was time for us to get off. Time to go to Drew's house. Time to take things to the next level.

Our walk from the station to his house was cold and short. We did not talk the whole way. There was this peaceful silence. Not awkward. Not unnerving. It was a peaceful silence.

Normally we would run considering the December conditions. Normally we would be chatting it up about anything. Normally we hold each other's hand or make small physical contacts throughout our walk. This time we just walked. In peace.

As soon as he unlocked the front door we were met with the warmth of his foyer. I had been to is house on numerous occasions. Again, our parents were old friends. Drew's house was much more spacious than mine. We had a one-story brownstone. His family had a two-story condo a bit closer to downtown.

He also had three younger brothers and a set of grandparents that lived in their house. The extra space was warranted. They had a dog that met us barking at the door. They also had a maid that was normally at the house.

"Hey where is Claudia?" I asked once I realized their house is rarely empty.

"Mom gave her the week off. She was barricaded with us the whole storm." He answered. "You need anything to drink or eat?"

"No I am fine." I was super nervous. Too nervous to eat or drink a thing.

"You want to play the game or watch something?"

"Uh, sure." I was completely confused now. I knew what we came to do. We both knew. I wondered why he wanted to play a game console all of a sudden.

"Ok let's go to my room," he said as he headed toward the stairs.

He had already taken off all of his winter gear. I was still fumbling with my snow boots. I was trying to be careful not to track mud and snow in the house. We did not have a maid. He was used to one. The way he just threw his belongings around haphazardly was indicative of that.

He disappeared up the stairs long before I finished. By the time I reached his room he had the TV blaring with the sounds of the game console. I walked past him and went to his bathroom. He had already started playing without me.

He shared a suited restroom with his younger brothers. It was a mess. I missed Claudia and I did not live there. The bathroom looked like it belonged to 3 boys.

After my potty break, I joined him in his room. "Hey you going to play the game until your parents come home?" My comment distracted him and he lost a game life.

"Maybe. Why? What you want to do?" He retorted smiling.

I just rolled my eyes. Thinking about it made my stomach flutter. Drew made my stomach flutter. I sat on his bed a just looked at him without saying a word.

He took the hint and put the game controller down. The winter sky where grey. The room was dark because his heavy blue drapes were drawn close. The game console's sound effects became the background music. He pulled off his shirt and joined me on his bed.

Drew played every sport he could fit in his schedule. He loved baseball. He had a lean baseball players body as evidence. He had six pack abs. He had thin, but very muscular arms.

I was nervous. I could tell he was too. He was normally confident and talking about himself. At the moment, he was as quiet as a mouse. We laid side by side touching each other's physical features.

He caressed my thick sandy hair while I rubbed the muscles in his arms. I was so used to him filling our silence, I decided it was my turn. The problem was, I had no idea what to say. I know what I wanted, just not how to articulate it.

He kissed me suddenly as if he could read my thoughts. I kissed him back. We kissed all the time, but this kiss was different. As we kissed, he pulled me closer to him. We were so close I could feel his heart racing.

Finally, I grabbed his drawstring shorts to pull him closer to me. I got so close I could feel it pulsate and scared myself. Instead of letting go, I grabbed it and began to caress it too. That sent Drew into a small euphoria.

He sat up on both knees and straddled me. He began slowly taking the rest of my close off. Kissing me every few inches he removed my clothing. I was flooded with a rush of emotions.

Part of me wanted to stop him before we got too far. Part of me was rooting for him to keep going. I did not say a word. I just let it happen.

Once he finished removing my garments he removed the rest of his. It was dark, but I could see it. I had seen it before, but never like it was at the moment. My glimpse was cut short by his next move.

He used his knees to spread my legs and laid on top of me. He kissed me a bit more. He touched me while we kissed until could feel it pulsating again. This time it was pulsating in my inner thighs.

He whispered "I love you", and entered me before I could respond. It was the worst pain I had ever felt in my life. But it hurt so good. I decided to keep going despite my nerve endings demanding I stop.

I felt even worse once he stopped. My legs felt like I had run a quarter mile. I wanted ice for my friend down below my waist. He cuddled me and kissed me once he cleaned himself up. I wanted him to leave me alone.

"What are you thinking?" He asked to break the ice after.

"That you just tried to kill me." I responded jokingly.

"Haha. Come on babe you know better than that. I would never hurt you."

"Well I have place on my body that feels differently."

"Really? What place is that?"

I just ignored his sarcasm. "I need to get going, my mom will be looking for me after a while. I did not tell her I was making a stop before I came home." I replied instead.

"Come on babe. Stay a little longer. My parents are at my brother's basketball game. My whole family is there. I missed it to spend time with you."

"I get it, but you know how my mom is."

"Yea, I know. She's so Holy and strict," he laughed.

"Watch it." I warned.

"Sorry, but when will I see you again, alone, before you go?" he demanded.

"I just don't know. I am helping my mom a lot to get ready."

"What about the party Saturday? You going?" He kept trying to confirm a time.

"I don't know yet." I wasn't giving him the answers he wanted. I could sense his rising frustration. I opted to leave instead of end the evening with a fight. "I am going to head home. I'll text you."

"You want me to walk you home?" he asked while I dressed.

"Yea." I said quietly. I really did not want him to. I wanted to be alone. I thought taking things to the next level would make life magical. It didn't.

I still cared about Drew. My life seemed to overshadow what we did though. I did not feel closer to Drew like I thought I would. I felt closer to my reality; Elgin, Texas.

As we walked towards my house, his love did warm me up. He held me while we walked. He told me how special I was to him. He even pleaded for me to stay in New York again.

I was flattered. I really was. However, I wanted to feel special to my dad. I wanted to be held by my dad. I wanted to go where ever my dad was. Drew and I shared a special moment together. I could not enjoy it thinking about my life.

When we arrived to my house he kissed me again. I would have normally invited him in, but our packed-up house was in shambles.

"Hey, you ok?" Drew inquired before they parted.

"Yea. Just a lot on my mind."

"See you tomorrow?" He wanted reassurance again.

"Yea."

"I love you," he said as a salutation.

"Alright." I said as I disappeared into my foyer from the winter winds.

Chapter 7: Skipping School

Part of me wished I could wake to the smell of my mom's breakfast daily. It was aroma therapy for me. It gave me energy and life. Instead of bacon all I smelled was imported coffee the next morning.

I was exhausted. I went to bed at a decent time, but I was still tired. I knew I only had a few more days to see my friends. I still had not told them I was moving out of state.

I physically and mentally did not want to deal with the reaction of it all. I was weighed down enough with my family coping. The energy for my friends just was not there. Despite it all, my baby sister remained oblivious and unscathed. I was glad about that.

I woke up to multiple text from Drew and notifications from other friends. Everyone was raving about the party Saturday night. All I could think about was the plane ride that was taking me to Texas until oblivion. Rather than ask my mom for money to party. I decided to just disappear to Texas.

"Mom." I had found her in the kitchen.

"Good morning love. Yes?" my mom said matter-of-factly.

"Sorry, good morning ma." I said and then hugged her tight. "Can I stay home?"

"Stay home? For what purpose?" She asked inquisitively.

"I'm stressed mom. My quarter grades are final. There is nothing more I can do in a couple of days. I just want to be alone."

"That is fair. You have been through so much in the past couple of weeks. Mama is so sorry. Things will get normal again for us soon. Will you help me get Judith to school? Maybe pack a bit while you are here?" She was trying to lighten the mood.

"No problem." I said as I poured a bowl of cereal.

Getting Juju ready for school was quite painstaking. I considered going to school even worse. I also did not want to face Drew. I felt awkward. We spent the night exchanging text and short calls. I actually appreciated him right now.

I just wanted my dad more than Drew. I wanted my dad more than a party. I wanted my dad more than hanging with my friends. My heart was broken.

I figured if I had my dad, things would go back to the normal how I wanted. I understood the move. I also understood selling our home and moving, meant we would not be coming home. That thought broke my heart a bit more.

The anxiety of not knowing made me frustrated. My feelings of my dad were conflicted. I also begin to resent him. I was raised to put family first. I felt like he chose heroin over us.

I could feel myself spiraling into a sea of negative thoughts. I just could not help it. My mom could read my gestures. She interrupted my thoughts.

"Hey can I take you to lunch since you will obliviously be my date today gorgeous?" she was smiling as she sipped her coffee.

"Uh, sure. You have a place in mind?" I asked taking my last bite of cereal.

"Yes actually. I was thinking we could eat at Nathan's." Her smile went from pleasantly sweet to devilish.

She knew me well, "Heck yes Mom!" I exclaimed.

Nathan's was my favorite burger spot. The establishment prided themselves on hormone and steroid free products. All foods were sourced from local organic farms. It was heaven on a bun. With bacon. Organic bacon.

I love cheeseburgers and fries. Mom was not too fond of my affection for the delicacy. She only allowed me to eat at Nathan's on special occasions or scarcely throughout the year. She preferred we at "healthy home prepared" meals. Part of me thought she was jealous of a little cooking competition swaying us.

There are hundreds of burger places in the New York area. Many of them offer quality ingredients. What made Nathan's special was the Owner. He was not some big shot making demands from a corporate office like most restaurants.

Nathan was the head chef of his own establishment. When he had time, he would come to the front of the house and greet customers. He had a way of making us feel like family. I had eaten there all my life with my mom. Juju was still young, and my mom tried to keep her away from certain foods. We would steal off together and indulge in fries.

"I'll go grab Juju ma." The invitation gave me a small boost.

As I headed down the hallway, I could hear my phone ringing. I was sure it was my friends looking for me before school. I kept going toward Judith. She was sound asleep.

"Juju, Good morning!" I said bursting into her room.

She did not move.

"Juju!"

Still nothing.

Finally, I yanked the covers from her bed. She curled herself in a fetal position and continued to sleep. I grabbed her feet and began to shake them. She hated that, but that was the only way I knew to wake her.

"Sttttoooopppppp it!" She demanded.

"It is time for school." I shot back.

"Noooooooo!" She whined.

I just did what I saw my dad do. Get her dressed as if she is saying nothing. He was pleasant like that. You could rant and rave, he would keep his course. So long as you ranted respectably.

After I managed to make her look cared for, I took her to the kitchen for breakfast. She was still pretty sour about being woken up. She refused to eat despite my warning it would be time to leave soon. As always, my mom signaled it was time to go, and Juju pitched a fit about eating.

Despite her fit, we were able to get her in the car and off to school. My mom announced my aunt was coming over to help finish packing. I still had a bit of my own room to pack. I decided I'd pack a bit more before heading to Nathan's.

Chapter 8: Texas

The next few days happened like a world wind. We packed as much as we could. All my aunts in New York saw us take off at the airport. It was a sad occasion. We were not leaving for a job promotion or vacation. We were leaving because my dad ruined our lives.

I felt the hate for my dad grow as the days past. I tried to suppress the hatred by reassuring myself things would get better. As we boarded our flight it hit me. We were really leaving. I officially hated my dad.

At first, I hoped he would come home soon. Then I just wished he would call. Next, I considered he would save us just before it was too late. But he did not.

I had not seen my biggest hero in weeks. I finally accepted that I probably never would. I did not want to see him anymore. After what he was putting us through I preferred he stayed away.

I spent most of the four and a half hours on the plane thinking about Texas. We visited my grandparents often, so I was familiar with it. I wondered about my new school. I wondered how I would make friend as a transfer from out of town.

I also wondered about my friends at home and school. Especially Drew. I decided it was best to leave without seeing him too. He was upset about it. However, he just had to get over it.

I would rather disappear without explanation than explain my dad loved heroin more than me. My mom did her best to make sure we were comfortable. Still, I could see the uncertainty in her eyes as well. In the midst of our personal mental battles, Juju was just excited to be on a plane. She was excited to see my grandparents.

As soon as we landed, my grandparents and my aunt Gina greeted us at the airport. Aunt Gina was my mom's oldest sister. She said she moved enough as a military brat, so she opted to stay in Texas when the rest of the sisters left the state for school. She was also my mom's prettiest sister. She was tall and had thick sandy hair like mine.

I was glad to have some where to possibly escape to besides my grandparents' house. Aunt Gina had no kids. I considered her rich. She lived alone in a big two-story home she purchased for herself. The houses seemed to be bigger in Texas too.

Most of our belongings were being shipped. We were able to grab our trip luggage and settle in quickly with my grandparents. They had plenty of space as well. There were rooms available for everyone to have their own. I decided to share with Juju instead.

All of my cousins and friends were up north. She was all I had. My phone rang excessively for the first few days I was in Texas. I did not have the courage to tell my best friends where I was or why. I choose to ignore the calls. My life was in Texas now.

My grandmother prepared a big dinner our first night home. We had fried chicken, collard greens, potatoes, mac and cheese, and host of accent dishes. It felt like a holiday. My only problem was there was nothing to celebrate. But the food was great.

"Mom thank you for this wonderful spread," my mom said as we finished our dinner.

"It is no problem. I was happy to cook for my girls," my grandma replied as she begian cleaning the table.

"We are glad you are home baby," my grandpa interjected, "I just wish it were under happier circumstances."

"I know dad, but we are here. We will make the best of the situation," my mom assured him.

"Well I am going to head out before any real cleaning starts." My aunt said jumping in their conversation.

"Typical. Get out of here you sloth!" My mom and aunt shared a laugh. "Seriously though G, can we chat before you leave?"

"Of course," my aunt answered wholeheartedly.
As they disappeared through the living room, I could hear the front door opening and closing. Whatever they went to talk about, my mom wanted the conversation to be private. But why? Before I could make phantom

assumptions, my grandma grabbed my attention.

"Hey you, how's Texas so far?" Her voice was soft and full of love.

"It is ok, I guess I will see in the days to come right?" I said not wanting to sound as bummed as I felt.

"I know this is a big adjustment. Your mom and aunts are used to moving from place to place. Your grandpa was a military pilot, we have lived in a few different countries. But I am worried about you. What are you really feeling?" She sensed my fakery.

My grandma was like my mom's clone. You could tell them it was alright, but they would pry until they received the truth. Judith and my grandpa went for ice cream. It was just us. I decided to just be honest.

"Grandma I don't want to be here. I want to be in New York graduating with my friends. I even have a cute boyfriend there. But I had to just leave! I felt like I left me!" Tears began to cumulate in my eyes.

"I know baby," my grandma replied as she reached to hug me.

I just let it out. I cried about all the things I was supposed to be strong about. I wanted to just get on a plane and head back. But to where? Our house was empty. I had made myself estranged to my friends on purpose.

"I am going to go get some fresh air grandma," I said forgetting my mom was outside, "I will help you clean up when I come back in."

"Ok baby." She just smiled a smile of concern.

I went out the back door. My grandparents had a huge lot of land. They had 20 or so acres behind their house. Being from New York, it was an abyss of darkness at night. Creepy. I was used to tall buildings and city lights illuminating the night.

I decided to circle around the house instead of taking on the abyss. As I neared the front of the house in search of light, I could hear my mom and aunt. Whatever they were discussing, it was intense. It almost sounded as if my aunt was chastising my mom.

I did not want to get too close. If I did they would hear my foot steps in the quiet night. Our new and nearest neighbors were ten minutes away. I had a thirty-minute drive to my new school. There was nothing but quiet and space out there.

"I am honestly disappointed you waited this long." I could hear my aunt saying.

"It is more complicated than you think. It is not something you just say. Especially right now!" My mom pleaded as a rebuttal.

"The longer you wait, the more damage is caused. Look at you! Things would be different if she just knew the truth. They both deserve that!" My aunt did not sound as if she bought my mom's excuse.

"Edith!" My grandma was calling from the back door. My mom and aunt heard her as well, I could hear them returning inside after her call.

I walked around nonchalantly, "yes grandma?"

"Will you make sure the lids are on the cans tight? Your grandpa is lazy and coons get in them if not." She was covered in dish suds.

"Huh," I was confused. I had no idea what a coon was. I also had no knowledge of the cans she was referring to.

"The trash cans baby. Right there on side of the house," she said pointing me in their direction.

My immediate thought was "you want me to touch garbage?" My immediate reaction was to "tighten the can lids". I respected my mom. I feared my grandma. She taught my mom how to skin a kid.

I could not help but wonder about my mom and aunt's conversation while obeying my grandma. After finding my dad, I could not put anything past my mom. She hid my dad's problem until it revealed itself. What else was she hiding?

I knew I could not ask her so I let it go. Instead, I became overcome with the thoughts of the next few days. My mom made it clear she did not support us missing much school. Before she started her new job, she set aside a few days to get us acclimated in school.

Part of me was ready for new friends. I was ashamed to tell my friends what had really happened. Disappearing seemed better than lying because they knew me. I figured if we stayed in New York, they would eventually find out the truth.

With a new place came new people. People that did not know I was forced from my brownstone by drugs. People that did not know I had a drug addict dad. People that would only know what I told them.

I was bothered that I would have to attend public schools though. I have spent my K-11 education in private facilities. I heard horror stories about the public schools. Things I could not fathom.

One time we heard there was a fight so bad at a public high school, a couple of people were stabbed. Another time we heard boys were busted smoking pot in the restroom. The worst story I heard was a public school principal was lit in fire. A kid threw alcohol on her and next a lit match.

Our parents always told us those kids were no different from us. They explained they grew up in different places so they act a "little" different. They made it clear we were to treat all people with respect. So, we respectfully ignored the public-school kids. Now I was about to be one of them.

Thinking about public school made my stomach hurt. Hopefully there were some cute boys there. Drew was cute, but he was also eighteen hundred miles away. A new state called for some new meat.

Chapter 9: The New Friend

Texas turned out to be bearable. I had to make adjustments, but it was less stressful than I thought. A few weeks after being there we started to hear from my dad again. Juju was ecstatic, I wasn't sure how to feel.

I thought when I spoke with him I would yell and blame him, but I did not. Hearing his voice put me at ease. I could also feel his guilt through the phone. He tried to reassured us things would return to normal.

Those promises made Juju happy. I think they made my mom hopeful. I wasn't buying it. Once an addict always and addict. Even though he was my daddy, he broke my heart. I would not allow that to happen again.

I would have loved to return to my brownstone. I just was not going to count on him to make that happen. We counted on him before. Now we are homeless in Texas.

After a few months, I had finished my junior year ninth in my new class. I hated it. I was fourth at my old school. I welcomed the summer and my new friends that came with it. There was not much to do in Texas but "hang out".

You remember that story I told you about public-school kids smoking pot in the restroom? That accusation is one hundred percent true. I might have even smoked a little bit myself. After all, I was a public student now.

"Edith! Is that you?!" My grandma followed me out of the kitchen.

"What? What are you talking about?" I asked disoriented. I was high and I could feel her getting ready to blow it.

"You smell like that stuff again!" She was livid. "This is the third time. I am trying not to stress your mother, but you are not going in the right direction."

"Grandma I hear you. This is the last time. Seriously." I was serious the last time she caught me too. I meant to be more discreet. Too late now.

Instead of responding she threw her hands up and retreated to her kitchen. I retreated to the room I shared with my five-year-old sister. She was at summer camp. I talked my mom into letting me stay home with my grandma. It was the first summer I was not enrolled in space, earth, or some academic camp.

I was glad about it. I liked hanging out with my new friends. They were a cool bunch. Down to earth. Looking to pass the time. Sometimes we did some things we should not have. Never too far from losing our morals.

My grandma hated my new friends. She said they were a group of "thugs" that distracted my studies. The smartest "thug" was ranked number three in our class. He was also very handsome. We had taken a liking to each other.

I wanted to go on the kitchen and grab some food. I just did not want to hear my grandma griping. My grandpa was with me the second time I was caught. He just laughed at her hysterics behind her back.

We also had a serious talk about the role drugs played in our moving. I understood where they were coming from. However, I was caught up with my "thugs" yet again. At least according to my grandma.

Since I could not get any food, I opted for the next best thing. A nap. I needed some energy before the Juju Bean returned home anyhow. She was ball of impulsive energy.

Sadly, my nap was abruptly interrupted. It was interrupted during the REM part. If it was not the REM that caused me to see stars during the interruption, it was my mom's hand. She woke me with a smooth strike and yank combo.

I was sitting up straight involuntarily. When I realized I was not dreaming, my mom was in my face. We were face to face. She was hot. As in mad, upset, enraged, and etc.

I spotted my grandmother standing behind her. She had her arms folded like a bouncer. I was surveying the room for an escape. My mom knew I would run. That is why she held my collar.

It was too early for her to be home. My grandma had her disapproving look to support my mom. I knew what this was about. My grandma was a rat. A bad one too. She returned to the scene of her snitchary.

"How dare you!"

I had never seen her that upset. I was not sure what to do. I was too scared to talk. I was too scared not to talk. I chose not to talk. I am glad I did, she had much to say.

"How dare you expose my parents, your sister, and me to that? Do you know what you are risking? You dare jeopardize what we have worked for! That is why I left your dad!" Tears begin to roll down her face.

"I love your father. I am an officer of the law. I had to choose between feeding you two or feeding him! I do not care what you are feeling there are legal ways to cope!" She released her clutch and left the room.

I felt bad. She was right. My grandma just stood there looking at me in disdain. I was not sure of how upset she was, I just remained silent.

Finally, she unfolded her arms, shook her head, and said, "Cheri is soft. I would have beat you." Then left the room.

I felt there was not much I could do at the moment. I laid back down. I unintentionally finished my nap. It was a good nap too. Despite their ranting.

When Juju returned home she jumped on me to signal the end of the good nap. She was a small thing, but her sharp elbows and knees were weapons. I gave her hugs and kisses until she wiggled away. It was nice to have good energy in the room.

The dim sunlight made me realize it was later than I meant to sleep. I was going back out to hang with my friends. I took a quick shower and change my clothes. The summer heat required frequent showers for me.

I was from New York. The climate acclimation had not happened yet. My grandma hated how many showers I took. It led her to suggest to my mom I should get a job and help. Not happening lady.

As time passed, my grandma grew to disapprove of many things. She thought my mom gave us "too much". She said we needed to "learn some responsibility". At least I had my grandpa.

He was more easy going. He would slip me money when she was not around. He was more understanding. I would talk to him when I felt down or stressed. He always had positive advice.

I grabbed a fanny pack and some shades to accent my outfit. We had plans to meet up at a gamers den. Eli loved video games so he went there often. I was excited to see him.

"Where are you going?" My mom stopped me as I was leaving the front porch.

"Uh, Game Caven." I was puzzled. I left all the time she never asked where. I just had a curfew.

"Do me a favor and get in the house." She retorted. She was still mad.

"Mom I won-"

"Shut up. I made a statement. I did not ask a question." Her teeth were clenched and her jaw was locked.

For my safety, I went back into the house. Know I was mad. She had already yelled at me. I did not understand why I could not go out.

I walked past the dining room where my family was eating dinner. I wanted to just go to my room. However, my grandpa called me back. Reluctantly, I turned around.

"Where you going?" He asked with a sincere smile.

"To my room grandpa," I could not hide my sullen mood.

"Stay, eat with us. I have not seen your pretty face today."

"Grandpa I wil-" I was so rudely interrupted.

"Sit down." My mom was behind me entering the dining room herself.

Now I was livid. I was hungrier than a homeless cat, but I did not touch a particle of food. I sat there and looked at my plate while they engaged in conversation. Juju squirmed and made protest about her vegetables. I wanted to be alone.

"Well, are you hungry darling?" My grandpa was on my getting nerves at this point.

"No sir." I said as politely as I could.

"She would rather be with those thugs. That's why she has a little attitude." My grandma smirked. Sometimes I wondered how my grandpa lived with her. They were complete opposites.

"Well that is done. With whom ever. You go nowhere without one of us. It is the summer. You are not driving to school. You do not need your car." My mom added.

"What? Because I smelled like a little weed? I am bound to this house? That is not fair!" They had taken everything. I might as well have had my say.

"You are being irresponsible. That trust needs to be built back." My mom replied.

"You guys are overreacting! Why can't I see my friends! I said I won't do it again!" I was ready to cry at that point. I really just wanted to see Eli.

"She really wants to see that boy," my grandma chimed in. She read my desperation well. She had also caught Eli and I hanging out behind her house multiple times. I must admit she kept some stuff between us.

"What boy?" My mom now had a new interest to light to flames over the pot.

Everyone was looking at me. Even Juju, she was excited no one was forcing her to eat vegetables anymore. She might as well have had popcorn for this show.

"What boy?" My mom asked again looking directly at me.

"We go to school together. We hang out some times." I said.

"Hang out where? Is this who you are doing drugs with?" She further inquired.

I did not want to say no, then I would be lying. I did not want to say yes, then she would surely ban me from seeing him. I just remained quiet. It seemed best at the time.

"Yes, it is." My grandma answered for me. I wished she was just a sweet old lady that minded her business. That is who she pretended to be at first.

"What, is it the guy you ran off a few months ago?" My grandpa just threw a monkey wrench.

"Months ago?" My mom was beginning to pick up on the information we had failed to make her privy to.

My mom worked long hours at her new job. She was deputy advisor for the county court system. My grandparents only told her unpleasant things they deemed necessary. Since moving to Texas, we spend more time with them than her.

"Yes Charles. That is the one." My grandma ignored my mom's concern.

"I think he was a fine young fellow. His head seemed to be on right when we spoke. I talked to him just before you ran him off. Matter of fact, he is smarter than her." My grandpa continued.

"Well how smart are they doing drugs?" My mom added.

My grandpa interrupted my mom, "Why don't we invite he and his folks for dinner. I like the guy."

"Absolutely not. She needs to be around better influences." My mom said rejecting his suggestion.

I just stayed quiet. I did not want him over for dinner. I did want to continue to see Eli. Hopefully my grandpa could make a tough enough case.

"Let's be honest. They are kids. Here is an opportunity to cultivate a relationship the right way. We can talk to their folks about the drug use. I just feel you will drive them together before you keep them a part. I have raised a few girls you know?" My grandpa responded as he took a bite of his food.

"You are right dad. I would love to speak with his parents about the drug use. You guys set something up." My mom smirked.

"Oh my God! We are not even dating! You guys are way over doing it!" It was time I spoke for myself.

"But he is your friend, right? Who has obviously been here before right?" My mom said sarcastically.

"Yes." Is all I said.

Chapter 10: Peace in the Truth

"Why do they want to meet my parents?" Eli asked incredulously. "My mom lives in Kansas, but my dad will probably do it." He said.

"Well, my grandma is convinced you are a "thug". My grandpa thinks you are a nice "fellow". My mom wants to know who I am hanging around. Maybe I went home smelling like pot too. You are the only friend my grandma has seen. You are guilty by association right now." I replied.

"Ok well I can see what he will say. That isno problem. I would want to know who my beautiful daughter was with too." Eli said as he tickled my thigh.

I still was not allowed to see Eli. We waited until after midnight to see each other. He would drive out to see me since my mom took my keys. He was so sweet.

Our night schedule worked out well. I was chained to home all day, so I slept. I woke up in the evenings to eat and meet Eli. We would talk on the phone when I was not sleep. We did not miss a beat despite my trouble. We got closer.

We were able to set a date on a Tuesday in June. His dad agreed to meet my family at a steakhouse in the city where I went to school. As we drew closer to the date, my mom lightened up. I was not allowed to go anywhere, but we did talk about things without her being upset.

I was able to receive her message more when things were less stressful. She was able to receive mine. She did not accept it still. She did receive it.

The dinner became more about getting to know my friend as we got closer too. At first it was a ploy for her to pry. Finding out about the pot made her more present and aware of what was going on. Even if she had to do it over the phone.

As the days past, Eli also mentioned that his dad appreciated my family's gesture. Time made me feel better about the meeting. I was still nervous though. Who knew what would be said at the table. I really like Eli. I did not want this dinner to ruin our friendship.

He seemed cool about it himself. He was always cool about everything. He had a level head no matter what was going on. I was used to explosive Drew. Eli was a breath of fresh air and peace in my crazy life.

The early morning before the dinner, Eli came over per usual. We hung out on the back porch in the summer night. I enjoyed seeing the stars at night. I did not have that luxury in the city. Sometimes on vacations.

We mostly talked about our senior year and plans we had. My grandpa was right, Eli was smarter than me. He was already taking college credited classes still in high school. He studied a lot and it showed.

He was the first guy to put studying before me. I kind of liked that. He was not perfect. But he felt perfect for me.

"I have a question for you." He said as we studied the sky.

"Yea? Ask on." I was interested in anything he said or did.

"Will you be my girlfriend? I know we just met this semester, but I can't help but want you to myself." He said shyly.

I was shocked. Of course I wanted to be his girlfriend! I just did not suspect he had the feelings I had. So, I suppressed mine. Him confirming it made me want to scream.

"Uh, yea sure." I said trying not to sound too excited.

"Well good. I thought I would make it official since we have that official family date later." He laughed jokingly.

"Yea, about that. I would rather not. I like my privacy. My mom stays in my business." I responded.

"Well, be grateful you have your mom. My mom left purposely. I wish she were here to be in my business. I wish she was here when I was thinking about how to ask you out." He said matter-of-factly.

"I hear you, and it is getting early. My grandma will be getting up in an hour." I said trying to break the serious mood our conversation took on.

His mom was a sore spot for him. He never told me exactly why. Just bits and pieces to let me know she was gone. Pieces to let me know she did not leave on a good note.

"Ok well can I have a hug before I go?" He chided back.

"Of course you can."

After seeing him off, I returned into the house. I took a shower and went to bed. I knew my family would be up soon. It was close to 5 am and alarm clocks started ringing at 5:30 am. Just as I am closing my eyes to sleep through the day.

————————————

When I woke up it was still a few hours before the dinner. I decided to take another shower before heading to the steakhouse. This was the first time I was meeting Eli's dad. I wanted to make a good first impression.

He had told me a lot about his dad. They were from the city. His dad grew up and stayed there. He worked as an accountant for a high-power firm. He also had investment properties. Like my aunt he was into real estate too.

Eli looked up to his dad a lot. He talked about him constantly. I felt like I knew more about his dad than him. I did not mind what he talked about. I just wanted to talk to him.

I imagined he looked like Eli. Maybe taller and weighed a little bit more. I knew he was pretty successful, so I did not want to seem basic. I picked out a modest outfit and used pearls to accent it.

My family arrive to the steakhouse before Eli and his dad did. Thanks to my grandma we left the house early. She contested we needed to be punctual. We were not going to embarrass her.

I was the one embarrassed. My first date with Eli as my boyfriend was with my grandparents. I was a little grateful still. Just a few weeks ago my mom forbade me to see him.

I watched the door anxiously. I was hoping everyone that came through the door was him. I had to reason with Juju to get the seat facing the entrance. I wanted to see him before he saw me.

When they did arrive, I hopped out of my chair to greet him. I could not help myself. I spent so much time hugging him I failed to even notice his dad. Mid hug, Eli peeled me away from him and said, "This is my dad Edwin Frank."

Realizing I was being rude, I stepped back and extended my hand. "Nice to meet you sir. May I take you all to our table?" I had found my manners.

As we walked to the table, something strange happened. My mom locked eyes with me, then her attention went to Eli and his dad. She appeared to give Mr. Frank a once over and her skin went pale. I mean he was good looking, but she acted as if she saw a ghost.

She excused herself from the table before we made it there. Mr. Frank grabbed my mom's arm as she brushed past us. She gave him a death look she would normally give us, and he immediately released her. We continued to the table and tried to have a normal dinner.

My grandparents made small talk with Mr. Frank while the waitress took drink orders. Eli entertained Juju and inquired about her interest. Normally I would have been jealous. I was too busy worried about my mom's reaction to Eli and his dad.

She took so long to return to the table that I went to look for her. She wasn't in the steakhouse lobby or outside. I checked the restrooms, she was not there either. Finally, I checked our vehicle.

There she was, in tears sitting in the driver side. I was immediately concerned and tried to console her. We sat there for a few minutes in silence. The only sounds heard were her soft sniffles.

Remembering my hot date was inside I said, "Mom what's wrong."

That made her cry harder. I felt horrible. I wondered if she was thinking about my dad. Maybe even the stress of moving was still bothering her.

"Babe just come out when you guys have finished dinner." She finally said.

"No mom, what's wrong? Have dinner with us!" I was confused.

"I can't."

"Why not?" I pressed.

"Edith, I will explain when we get home." She continued to cry. "Please just allow me to be alone."

"Well I will tell them we have to go." I decided.

"No just eat and enjoy yourself." She responded.

"Mom I won't go back in without you." I was beginning to cry myself. My mom's overwhelming sadness was hitting me. Almost the same way it seemed to hit her in the restaurant.

There was a long pause. Then she said, "Edith I need to tell you something."

"Yea?"

"You cannot date Eli anymore. He's your-" her words were cut short by her tears.

"My what?" I was beyond interested now.

"Your brother." She managed to get out before she broke down again.

"Brother." I whispered to myself.

For him to be my brother we would have to share parents. That confused the hell out of me. I know my mom is my mom. I was practically her twin. I know my dad is a heroin addict in a residential treatment center. I needed her to elaborate.

"What do you mean mom?" I inquired.

She took a deep breath, "Kerry is not your father. Edwin is."

I felt faint. She had to be joking. "Mom are you serious?"

"Edith, Edwin and I went to high school together. We saw each other sometimes when I came home from New York during college breaks. One break I went back to New York, my senior year of law school, I went back pregnant with you. Your dad was so excited, I did not have the heart to tell him you were not his."

She put her hands to her face and cried more.

"Wait so Mr. Frank is like, your boo?" I asked.

"No. Not anymore. And he was with Eli's mom at the time. So, he was never "mine". I broke things off once Kerry knew I was pregnant. But, Edwin is aware of you. He was adamant I kept you. He has just never seen you." She seemed devastated.

If she was not, I was. I wondered what in my life was the truth at this point. My dope fiend dad was not really my dad. Public school was not so bad.

What hurt me is that after all we had been through, I thought in Eli I had found peace. Just like everything else in my life, that peace was disrupted. Not because of malice, but because of fate. At least I found out the truth before I gave him a piece of me.

Builder's Code Excerpt

If you put yourself in a race with 8 people someone will place first, second, third, and so on to eighth. Now you have to decide now if you are going to be honest with yourself or not. If you are not, let me remind you most poor 50-year olds haven't been honest with themselves in 50 years. Close the book, stop the audio, or diminish whatever medium you are using to receive this literature.

Honesty, honest, and honesty, will be your best friend in the journey to becoming a better person and escaping your undesired environment. If you cannot instantly articulate the definition of honesty. Stop receiving this literature and look up the definition. You definitely possess some inkling of the character trait of honesty, if not you wouldn't have continued to receive this message.

Now, say these words out loud; I WILL BE 50 YEARS OLD, WHAT DO I WANT TO HAVE BY THEN? Let's revisit the 8 people that start at the same race. Think of your classmates, siblings, everyone in the world born on the same day as you, where are you compared to them? Many philosophers, theologians, educators and others will contend that you shouldn't compare yourself to others.

They support the you should "Run your own race" cliché. This is a half-sided message. These same respected classes have to at some time admit they compared themselves to someone else. However, when they compared themselves it was with the humbleness of self-reflection, not the haughtiness of jealousy. It seems easier however to tell the masses to "focus on yourself and don't compete with others".

Compare, compete, and challenge others; with tact. Comparing, competing, and challenging is an internal tool that drove the greatest; be it athlete, real estate baron, or president. The idea may be radical, but let's review the facts by using first names only; Steph, Roman, Serena, and Oprah. This list of proven winners has 3 things in common; they knew how to compare, compete, and challenge. These words naturally incite, the character traits of jealousy, spite, and deception (a negative form of strategy) in people that aren't honest with themselves.

Honest people compare themselves without desire for the holdings of other. They simply say "we are the same age, and I didn't do as much as I could've with the time allotted to me. NOW, what can I do to increase my own productivity and possibilities?"

Honest people compete by strategizing ways to increase their holdings and follow through with the plan. They simply say " NOW that I acknowledge what the process is to realize the fruit of my productivity, am I executing the process? What is going well? What do I need to improve?" Honest people challenge others by making sure they are working as hard as others or harder. They simply say "If he had to talk to 10 clients to close with one, I need to talk to 100 clients to close with ten." The law of numbers.

The opposite of honesty is dishonesty. When dishonest people compare, compete, and challenge others, they say just the opposite to themselves compared to those that are honest. When they compare they say, "I'm not where I should be because my parents aren't rich". Instead of competing, they fail to adequately plan, prepare, and execute. When presented with competition they fail and say "I was so tired after work I did not have time to start a part time business, NOW inflation has made my retirement check insufficient substance". In the face of challenges, they simply retreat. Dishonesty is a character trait you should discard from your personal, professional, and mental realms.

In the spirit of honesty, answer the following questions:

Have I achieved ALL that I could have by now? Why (Without blaming others.)

What can I do to start achieving ALL that I can?

One reality you should be honest with yourself about now is that you will be old. There are some people that are blessed to be able to work until the day the die. As a matter of fact, some people choose to work until the day they die. But here is another half-sided message. There is a difference between going to work every day because you WANT TO and because YOU HAVE TO. Many people all over the world find themselves working because they HAVE TO.

In 2017, Bloomberg published an article title "Working Past 70: Americans Can't Seem to Retire (U.S. seniors are employed at the highest rates in 55 years)"[1] As companies moved away from benefit pension plans that promised a steady income to the beneficiary until death during retirement, contribution plans are changing the dynamics of how one retires and when. If one does not plan fiscally responsible for their retirement, they could find themselves looking for a job on the other side of retirement if their contribution plan dries.

When one does minimal financial planning, they do create some type of safety net for themselves to retire, but sometimes do not take into account the unexperienced happen stances of getting older. For example, a retiree may have financially planned all they knew how to be secure as a retiree, but they did not take into account sickness or terminal illness. Certain diseases like cancer, heart disease, and brain procedures can have costly treatments that are not covered by all insurances. When they retire the first start out

[1] Steverman B. (2017) Working Past 70: *Americans Can't Seem to Retire* U.S. seniors are employed at the highest rates in 55 years. Bloomberg. Retrieved from https://www.bloomberg.com/news/articles/2017-07-10/working-past-70-americans-can-t-seem-to-retire

as healthy and vibrant, they may not enroll in more expensive and covering plans in order to cut cost as they adjust to a retired life.

If a bank account draining sickness or occurrence does happen, they find themselves pulling from the very sea of money that was meant to secure the rest of their waking days. In efforts to replace or recover the money they find themselves looking for work or moving in with loved ones if they are not able to return to physical labor. These are not uncommon occurrences among the minimally financially prepared classes. Yet countless generations fall victim to the cycle.

The impoverished and some middle class tend to shy away from the topic of retirement. This is either because they are sold that the government will supplement their retirement, they have not considered inflation, or that they may outlive their contributions. Contributions are monies set aside in a savings account that matures with tax incentives usually dispersed incrementally to retirees. There are times when they are taken out in lump sums for health purposes, debt reduction, and other likely emergencies. Some retirees are honest with themselves and make a last-ditch effort take their contributions and produce more income. Some are successful and some are not.

One point of reference of a ditch effort was from a retiree on the MSNBC network show The Profit. He appeared on the show as an effort to save his failing business. While taping, he divulged that he desperately needed the business to work because he used his retirement money as the startup investment. He did not say "I realized that my retirement may not be enough. I did not want to go back to being a full employee. So, I used my retirement to start a business." However, this is a common occurrence.

Based on statistics collected by the U.S. Bureau of Labor Statistics, "the self-employment rate among workers 65 and older is the highest of any group in America" (Hipple S. and Hammond L. 2016) [2]. This is not to say that all self-employed retirees are broke and struggling retirees. Some live thriving lives by investing and building businesses for the thrill

---

[2] Hipple S. and Hammond L. (2016) Self-employment in The United States. U.S. Bureau of Labor Statistics Spotlight on Statistics Pg.5 https://www.bls.gov/spotlight/2016/self-employment-in-the-united-states/pdf/self-employment-in-the-united-states.pdf

of making money and not to afford needed prescriptions. It needs to be pointed out that there is a such thing as poor financial planning and dooming oneself to a life of working simply to survive instead of actually living if one is not careful.

One has to be fair and point out that with the advancements in medicine and technology, Americans are living longer. Along with living longer they also are able to maintain a more stable shell in their older age if they take proper care and groom themselves throughout their lives. However, many are in the workforce to supplement their shrinking income and growing needs. In 1994 only 8% of Americans 70-74 were still active in the labor force. By 2017 the percentage has rose steadily to 19% and climbing for those that are physically able, according to a Bloomberg article[3].

Working through what were once retirement ages is becoming so common that there are talks of legislation to protect the

---

[3] Bloomberg N.A. Working Past 70: *Americans Can't Seem to Retire*. Bloomberg. Retrieved from https://www.bloomberg.com/news/articles/2017-07-10/working-past-70-americans-can-t-seem-to-retire

rights and give recognition to older people in the work place. (Lee 2015)[4] There is no secret that hiring an older person in the work place comes with hidden expenses and fees like a payday or cash advance loan. They are more likely to miss shifts due to illness or mandated appointments. They are physically, not all the time, less efficient than a younger employee. The list goes on, and as a hiring manager, unless they have the most outlandish educational background and are in pinnacle shape, it is easy to justify hiring a younger candidate.

The rapid evolutions of technology and systems are another hindrance for older people attempting to enter into the workforce. There are some bad great grandmothers that can whip out their smartphone and send a text faster than their grandchildren. There are some hot grandpas in the world that think technology is better than Mrs. Baird's Bread because he can keep in touch with his girlfriends. Then there is that percentage of the population that refused to acclimate and keep up with the ever-changing technology.

---

[4] Lee G. (2015) The Age of No Retirement. Creative Review. Vol. 35 Iss. 6. pg. 26-30

Or they did not obtain a formal degree or vocational training in their younger years. Trying to obtain new skills and education presents itself as one of the biggest obstacles when running against some younger counterparts for a position.

There are new industries evolving, such as Lyft and Favor, that open the door to earn supplemental income. Retirees can complete simple task like picking up food for clients, or running cab routes in major cities with little to no effort. So, there are opportunities out there. But who wants to get to the end of their life and serve out of necessity? Then there is a dark threat of these industries called Artificial Intelligence. At the rate that Elon Musk is going, robots will use their jetpacks to deliver food and goods to clients. Heavier orders are moved by Artificial Intelligent Semi Delivery trucks. Imagine being asked in an interview at 75, "Why should I hire you above a robot I will eventually get for free through tax breaks and deductions?" Who really has the right answer for that?

When contributions run out for some, they turn to family to help with their balances. This comes in many forms. Parents moving in with children to save or supplement their income after their property taxes became too expensive. Children or the government providing funding for nursing homes or community fees. Older siblings moving in together to decrease living expenses.

All of these things are hailed as labors of love, which is important, but honestly, what about laboring for 10 years to save your loved ones 30 years of burdens? Along with providing yourself with 40 years for happiness? There are circumstances in life that are out of human control. There are those that are born with deficiencies and roadblocks that only God can control. However, if you are in taking this particular literature, these are probably not descriptors of you. Or they are and you're honest your ability to persevere despite adversity. For that I love you.

For those not plagued with debilitating adversities, why plague your loved ones with later burdens you can alleviate right now? Let's be honest, if you drive a $1000 cash car and cancel the next 4 years of vacations, you could probably own a rental property that will pay you income from now to death whether you wake up at 5:30 am or noon. Those that are ill prepared for retirement have many commonalities.

They tend to spend on wants before they pay for needs.

Be honest; do you get that new pair of shoes or watch the day you get paid and pay the water bill after the due date?

They tend to satisfy present desires instead of future security.

Be honest; do you buy yourself and at times lunch for your coworkers? Knowing, one loaf of bread, one pack of turkey, and preferred condiment cost around 10 bucks a week?

They also tend to own more depreciating items than assets in order to impress others. This is the most common among the impoverished.

Be honest; do you have a nice car with a note attached, rented luxury apartment, but not income bringing assets? The darker side of the two are the impoverished. They typically have spent a decent amount of time subsidizing their lifetime with government assistance.

I was personally guilty of everything that is listed above. That is why I am very familiar with the causes and outcomes. I did these things instinctively because of my exposure and so do many others. In order to reach their desired environment, one has to let go of unprofitable things and habits. They distract and prolong the journey to the desired environment.

Since they don't possess retirement contributions to deplete, the ill prepared frequent nursing homes that accept government insurance and incentives. They also tend to live independently being a recipient of government housing, food, and healthcare for a lifetime. Again, there are some that are in justifiable need of these services. However, there is a substantial number of those that are not. They don't address or prepare for retirement because they simply don't see the need to.

If one were born after the 1970's they had have little no knowledge of the harsh realities of surviving times like the Great

Depression. During the Great Depression, one only had possession of what they out right owned. This was a financially tumultuous time that subjected many Americans to using whatever was on hand for housing for their families like cardboard or scrap metal. In 1932 alone "273,000 people lost their homes." (Siracusa & Coleman, 2002, pg. 26)[5] Thanks to government initiatives and assistance there is no longer a fear for Americans not working to sustain themselves.

Housing, Medical, and other government sponsored programs have blinded new generations since the 1930s. These programs were meant to help the fallen man pick himself up and began to provide for his family again. Instead it has erupted into oceans of money flowing to able body Americans making the conscious decision not to work and sustain themselves. There are some that make an effort to find employment, but if not rapidly attained they easily turn to the helping government hand. They fail to come to the realization that we live in a free

[5] Siracusa J. & Coleman D (2002) Depression to Cold War: *A History of America from Herbert Hoover to Ronald Reagan* Perspectives on the Twentieth Century. Pg. 26

enterprise nation that gives them the ability to create their own source of unlimited income.

If the government had enough citizen and legislative support to roll back most of the government assistance programs initiated almost 90 years ago, many Americans would find themselves in dire circumstances. Census.gov reports that "52.2 million American participate in government assistance programs." That is 52 million people that would have to literally "figure it out". The Great Depression occurred due to issues like redlining, rise in low qualifying buyers, and life circumstances that are not keeping up with the dropping dollar. If one were to compare the nation's financial forecast to now and the start of the Great Depression, they might find more similarities than differences. If banks and credit companies began demanding loans are accelerated to financially support their institutions, millions of Americans will be "out on the streets".[6]

---

[6] The US Census (2015) 21.3 Percent of U.S. Population Participates in Government Assistance Programs Each Month. Retrieved from https://www.census.gov/newsroom/press-releases/2015/cb15-97.html

There are those that are sufficiently prepared and fully enjoy their retirement. Instead of being the parents living with the "good kids", they are requested to visit or take on babysitting expeditions while their children enjoy themselves. They spend the second half of their life traveling, hunting, shopping, or whatever their heart desires. The impoverished and lower middle class previously described usually have a negative perspective of the "sufficiently prepared".

They see the harvest of the sufficiently prepared and do not take into account that sowing preceded that fruit. If they did, they'd be so occupied pulling in their own harvest that they wouldn't be able to consider their neighbor's.

For those that work in a corporate setting or for a large organization, especially salaried workers, they are offered company sponsored or partnered retirement plans and options. Some organizations even offer opportunities for the employee to purchase ownership in the company through stocks and certificates. But no one in certain geographical regions are walking around with banners that read "Your Retirement is Near, Plan Now!".

Even though they should. Many do not take the time to face the harsh realities of retiring unprepared until they attempt to retire; unprepared.

The impoverished, the middle class, and the sufficiently prepared all have one thing in common; they will be old. Be honest, how old are you? Which category of the three do you most relate to? Where are you on the timeline of your retirement? Are you on track to burden your kids with your old age expenses or to free them to enjoy the life you helped them build? Some answering this question will be honest with themselves and they are on track and sufficiently prepared. There are also some that will be honest with themselves and they are not on track or sufficiently prepared.

If you are not prepared or on track to be, take the time now to make a very important decision like I had to do. This is the very first phase of freeing yourself from your undesired environment. Do you want to be on track and sufficiently prepared? If yes continue reading or listening, if not as before; Close the book, stop the audio, and stop receiving this literature. Begin now by identifying your personal goals and wants. Goal setting is a treasure map for ones' life. Goal accomplishment is the treasure of one's life.

Goal setting can be easy to define, but goal accomplishing is a whole other beast by itself. Many social people that hold healthy conversations are able to articulate the things they have and want to accomplish during their lifetime. Rarely do they expose all of the areas and ideas that were the epitome of their failures and how they coped if they coped at all. These are the wounds people need to see. If everyone honestly revealed their deepest ambitions, one will find that there are many millionaire souls, but fewer millionaire finishers.

Not all doomed retirees walk blindly into doom. Some can comprehensively understand what they need to secure the desired environment they would have for themselves. At the same time, they are just unwilling to be creative and innovative in a capacity that will help them fulfill their future desires. They purposely live day in and day out knowing they are not putting their best selves forward to secure happiness. They wake up daily with the intention of the government or a loved one supporting them in their geriatric years.

Future planning requires one to be actively engaged in an ongoing process that can take decades to reach the expected end. It would seem as if since 100% of Americans are subject to retire, that 100% of Americans would be actively seeking retirement advise. Granted that 100% is skewed by sickness, accidents, and other circumstance in life. Those that are healthy and cannot identify any perceived obstacles to retirement should be prepared. However, number shows that less than 15% of retirement participants seek retirement advise. (Barney 2017)[7] This is of those with retirement plans, the numbers are worse if you factor in the number that do not have a plan.

In order to craft their start, one has to be honest about their end and what it takes to get there. Being honest would require one to look at the cost of the process and the weight of the load. One has to understand realistic time tables and be disciplined to keeping to

---

[7] Barney L. (2017) Only 13%of Retirement Plan Participants Seek out Advice. Plan Advisor. Retrieved from https://www.planadvisor.com/13-retirement-plan-participants-seek-advice/

schedules. It is imperative to manage risk by envisioning the not so pretty side like "what if I get sick during retirement", and put in place safe guards to protect their assets in hard times. One has to be open to learning and a friend of exposure to be able to weigh all plausible options. One has to let go of inhibitions while they visualize their honest and desired end.

About the Author

Toy Taylor is a native of Waco, Tx. She currently manages a behavior unit in Austin, Tx. For more information and other works by the author please visit toytaylorbooks.com.

www.ingramcontent.com/pod-product-compliance
Lightning Source LLC
Chambersburg PA
CBHW030301130626
46549CB00002B/633